PRINCE NOT-SO CHARMING

Her Royal Slyness

Roy L. Hinuss

Illustrated by Matt Hunt

[Imprint]
MAKE YOUR MARK

[Imprint]
MAKE YOUR MARK

A part of Macmillan Publishing Group, LLC
175 Fifth Avenue, New York, NY 10010

Library of Congress Control Number: 2017958058

ISBN 978-1-250-14240-5 (paperback) / ISBN 978-1-250-14239-9 (ebook)

Our books may be purchased in bulk for promotional, educational, or
business use. Please contact your local bookseller or the Macmillan
Corporate and Premium Sales Department at (800) 221-7945 ext. 5442 or
by e-mail at MacmillanSpecialMarkets@macmillan.com.

Book design by Ellen Duda

Illustrations by Matt Hunt

Imprint logo designed by Amanda Spielman

First edition, 2018

1   3   5   7   9   10   8   6   4   2

mackids.com

You swiped this book? Oh, you will pay.
I'll curse you each and every day!
I hope your nose grows twice in size!
I hope your butt lures biting flies!
May rats poop on your ice-cream cake!
May every eyelash start to ache!
I'll shout and shout till I turn blue:
"May someone swipe nice things from YOU!"

For Queen Mom and King Dad

CHAPTER 1

"Whoa! Whoa!"

Prince Carlos Charles Charming could feel droplets of perspiration forming on his brow. He clenched his teeth. His eyes flashed with panic. His ankles began to shake.

"Whoooa!" he yelled.

Carlos's words bounced against the walls of the empty ballroom, so as he yelled "**whoooa**," a bunch of **whoooa**s yelled back at him.

It was a little disorienting. And now was *not* the time to be disoriented.

As Carlos **whoooa**-ed and wobbled, Jack

the Jester sat crisscross applesauce upon a large purple velvet pillow. Jack nodded, making the bells on his red-and-green hat jingle-jangle.

Carlos found the jingle-jangling disorienting, too.

"You're doing fine, kiddo," Jack said. "Just relax. Just keep moving."

"I-I don't know if I *can* relax!" Carlos sputtered. "Every time I move, I— **WHOA!**"

"Whoa, whoa, whoa, whoa . . ." the walls replied.

It was as if Carlos was relearning how to walk, which was pretty much what he was doing.

"Let the stilts become part of your body," Jack instructed.

Weaving on his shaky stilts, Carlos blinked a drop of sweat out of his eye. "Is it hot in here?"

"That's stress sweat, boy," Jack said. "Don't worry. You're only three feet off the ground."

Carlos's feet may have been only three feet off the ground, but his head was *eight* feet off the ground. And it felt much, *much* higher. Also, the feet at the end of his new, unsteady legs were not his normal size-nine shoes but two skinny poles no thicker than a silver dollar.

The very thought made him dizzy.

Don't think about it, don't think about it, don't think about it, Carlos thought.

But trying not to think about it made Carlos think about it even *more*.

"Don't lose focus," Jack warned.

But the sweat, tension, and dizziness made Carlos less focused than ever.

"Keep moving," Jack said.

Carlos took a step, but his stilt couldn't find the floor. He felt his weight shift. He felt himself fall. He caught a glimpse of the stone floor rushing up to meet his face.

PUH!

Oh! That fall was kind of pleasant, Carlos thought. *I didn't know stone floors could be so comfortable.*

He blinked once, then twice. He found his head resting on a large pillow made of purple velvet. His eyes flicked to where Jack the Jester sat, though Jack wasn't sitting anymore. He was on his feet, with his left arm outstretched before him, as if he had just released a bowling ball.

"Thanks for letting me borrow your pillow," Carlos said.

"Thanks for falling where I threw it!" Jack replied. "Your parents have enough problems with our jester lessons. I don't think they'd like it if I returned you to them with a dented head."

Carlos's parents, Carmine and Cora Charming, were the king and queen of the peaceful and happy land of Faraway Kingdom. That meant Carlos was a prince. That *also* meant that Carlos was expected to do princely things.

Jestering was pretty much the opposite of being princely, but Carlos loved it. And King Carmine and Queen Cora were good parents as well as good rulers. So they allowed the jester lessons to continue as long as jestering didn't interfere with Carlos's royal responsibilities.

Jestering, they told him, must only be a hobby. A very private, very *secret* hobby.

But jestering was more than a hobby to Carlos. It was his passion. And he was good at it, too. For the most part.

"You need a little more practice with the stilts, I see." Jack jingle-jangled over to where Carlos lay. He offered a hand, but Carlos didn't take it.

"Can I just lie here for a minute?" He was comfortable on the floor and still a little woozy.

"Sure." Jack smiled down at his student. "You earned a break. Would you like a little water?"

"Yes, thank you," Carlos said.

The flower on Jack's vest sprayed water in Carlos's face.

"HA-HA! Gotcha!" Jack wheezed with laughter.

Carlos dried his face on his sleeve and shook his head. *How did I fall for that old gag?* he thought.

Nonetheless, Carlos couldn't help but smile.

Jack plopped himself down on the stone floor. He was the only adult Carlos knew whose knees never made cracking noises. The jester scratched his chin and studied Carlos's face. "You do look a little glassy-eyed," he admitted. "Tell me a poop joke."

"Why?" Carlos asked.

"Poop jokes make the mind sharp," Jack said.

"They do?" Carlos asked.

Jack shrugged. "How should I know? I just wanna hear a poop joke."

"Okay. . . ." Carlos tried to come up with a good one. "What do you call a fairy using the toilet?"

"What?" Jack asked.

"Stinker Bell."

Jack's brown cheeks stretched into a wide, merry grin. His dark eyes crinkled with delight. He let out a long, appreciative laugh. "That's a good one! You, kid, are a natural jester."

It was Jack's highest compliment, but Carlos couldn't fully accept it. "I don't know, Jack," he said. "I've been working with stilts for a month, and I still can't get the hang of them."

"You will," Jack assured him. "You got the hang of everything else."

This was true, but somehow stilt-walking was *different* from everything else. Every time Carlos got up on the stilts, his eyes would get blurry and he'd start to shake. No matter how much he practiced, the feelings never went away.

"You're a fine jester, Carlos. And I'm not the only one who thinks so." Jack raised a mischievous eyebrow. "In fact, I have *news*."

Jack paused, letting the word *news* hang there for a moment to give it a little extra oomph. He peered over his shoulder. He lowered his voice. In Fancy Castle, spies could be anywhere. "Wanna work on your hobby in the village tonight?" he asked.

Carlos's eyes brightened. "You *know* I do," he whispered. "When, where, and what?"

"Five o'clock, Village Hall, the Zimmerman bar mitzvah," Jack said.

Carlos's heart leapt. "Five o'clock. Hm. I think I can sneak out." His stilt-walking worries faded away. "One way or another, I *will* sneak out. I am *so* there."

Jack winked. "It'll be our little secret."

"And the Zimmermans' secret." Carlos winked back.

"And their fifty guests' secret." Jack chuckled.

"And the secret of the one hundred guests at last week's Stravini wedding." Carlos chuckled louder.

"And the secret of the thirty guests at little Bobby Vapors's birthday party two weeks ago." Jack snorted.

"And the secret of everyone at the grand opening of Corky's Pre-Owned Catapults." Carlos snorted louder.

"And the secret of everyone at the annual Moat-Diggers' Convention!"

"And the secret of everybody at the Renaissance Faire!"

"And the—" Jack began.

"And the—" Carlos began.

But Jack and Carlos were unable to continue. They were too busy laughing.

To put it another way, Carlos and Jack's secret wasn't *much* of a secret. In fact, nearly *everybody* in Faraway Kingdom knew that Carlos secretly worked as a freelance jester.

Only two people didn't know: King Carmine and Queen Cora. If they found out, Carlos would probably be grounded forever. So every farmer, villager, merchant, and aristocrat in Faraway Kingdom kept their yap shut whenever the royal family was within earshot.

"What are the Zimmermans looking for?" Carlos asked.

"A little of everything," Jack replied. "But mostly juggling."

"Cool," Carlos said. Juggling was his specialty.

Carlos began to work out his routine in his mind. However, he was soon distracted by a rapid series of approaching clickita-clickitas.

"Hark! What's that noise?" Jack made sure his voice was loud enough for the owner of the clickitas to hear. "Is that Fancy Castle's new puppy?"

Jack winked at Carlos. Carlos grinned.

The clickitas stopped abruptly and were replaced with a small, impatient "Harrumph."

"Here puppy, puppy!" Jack called.

"I keep telling you and telling you! I am *not* a puppy," responded the distant voice. "I am a *dragon*!"

"A dragon?" Jack asked. "Are you sure?"

"Yeeeeeeees!" the voice said.

More clickitas echoed down the hall. Moments later, Smudge galumphed into the ballroom.

Smudge was indeed a dragon. He had colorful scales, bat wings, a long tail, and sharp black talons that clickita-ed on the stone castle floors. The only thing about Smudge that wasn't very dragonish was his

personality. Smudge had a lot more in common with a golden retriever than with a ferocious beast.

"See?" Smudge said. "Dragon!" To prove it, he let out a huge **ROOOOAR!**

Jack nodded. "Oh, yes! I see it now." Normally, Jack wouldn't stop teasing someone so soon after he got started, but teasing Smudge was a lot like teasing a toddler—it didn't take long before the jokes stopped being funny and started being mean. "You, Smudge, are clearly *not* a puppy."

Smudge nodded. "Dragon. A little boy dragon. Don't forget next time, okay?"

"I won't," Jack promised. But, of course, he *would* forget, because forgetting is funny.

Jack gave Smudge a little skritch under his chin, making the dragon purr a puff of smoke. Smudge could hardly ever resist a skritch, but he steeled himself. He had a job to do. He pulled himself away from Jack and clickita-ed to Carlos's side.

"Oh, hai, CC!" Smudge chirped. "You sleeping?" (Carlos was still lying on the velvet pillow.)

"No," Carlos said. "What is it?"

"Mama wants you," Smudge said.

Carlos tried to stifle a weary sigh but didn't do a very good job of it. "What does she want?"

"Something about being princely," Smudge said.

Carlos's sigh was replaced with a groan

so loud that the ballroom groaned back at him. He sat up and began to untie his stilts. "I hate prince training."

"No, you don't," Smudge protested.

"Yes, I do." Carlos tossed the stilts aside, allowing them to smack the stone floor with a satisfying clatter. He pulled himself up into a standing position. His knees cracked.

"But if you didn't have prince training, we wouldn't be bestest friends!" Smudge said.

This was true. Carlos met Smudge on his very first prince assignment. Now the dragon lived full-time at Fancy Castle, lighting chandeliers with his fiery breath, organizing

a knitting club with the housekeeping staff, and accepting cuddles wherever he could find them. (Smudge found cuddles pretty much everywhere.)

"So . . . so . . . so maybe something fun will happen this time, too!" Smudge went on.

"Maybe," Carlos said, although he didn't really believe it. "At least I won't be falling off of stilts."

"It *will* be fun, CC," Smudge decided. "And I'll come with you! I make things funner."

"Yes, you do," Carlos agreed.

"And maybe we'll even meet a new bestest friend!" Smudge said.

Carlos scratched Smudge's head. "Maybe," he said.

And, with a quick parting wave to Jack the Jester, the two of them toddled off to find the queen.

CHAPTER 2

Queen Cora was in the throne room—a room large enough to hold a half dozen normal-sized houses. As Carlos and Smudge passed through the entrance, they saw her by the far wall. She was wedged into her golden throne with her silken robes, capes, and petticoats carefully and colorfully arranged around her like a peacock's tail. A small group of servants stood by the queen's side, ready to address her every need.

Queen Cora was a big woman with an even bigger personality, but even she had some difficulty getting her voice to carry the length of the throne room. She cupped her large, tan hands around her mouth before offering a greeting.

"HELLOOOOOOO! COME CLOOOOSER!"

Carlos and Smudge did as they were told, padding down the long ribbon of red carpet to where she sat.

"Smudgie!" Queen Cora beamed with

HELLOOOOOO!

delight. "You found Carlos just like I asked you to! You are such a good little dragon!"

Smudge's tail whipped back and forth in reply, but its joyful motion didn't quite match up with the grave expression on his face.

"It was really tricky to find him," Smudge said, nodding. He made his eyes big and adorable.

"It was tricky?" the queen asked.

"It was *reeeeally* tricky," Smudge continued. "I searched and searched. I was going to give up, but I kept searching so you'd be happy."

"Well, I *am* happy!" the queen said. "I am so happy with your good work that I think I'll give you a treat!"

The dragon's tail now whipped back and forth so fast that it smacked against Carlos's shin.

"Ow! Dang it!" he exclaimed.

"Would you like a fudgesicle?" the queen asked. "I bet you would like a— **OOF!**"

Queen Cora didn't say Smudge would like an **OOF.** Queen Cora said **OOF** because Smudge leapt into the queen's lap. The queen recovered quickly, however. "Oh, aren't you an affectionate angel!"

She nodded to her handmaiden, who presented Queen Cora with an unwrapped fudgesicle.

Smudge flopped onto his back, opened his toothy mouth, and accepted a bite.

Carlos rolled his eyes. "Smudge can hold his own ice cream, Mom."

"Oh, I know," the queen cooed, but she showed no sign of handing the fudgesicle to Smudge. Instead, she rubbed the dragon's pudgy belly and waited for him to signal that he was ready for another bite.

He opened his mouth wide. "Aaaah!" That was the signal.

Carlos couldn't help but roll his eyes again. "What do you want me for, Mom?"

"Hm?" Cora looked up from Smudge as if waking from a deep sleep. "Oh! Carlos! Yes! I have terrible, terrible news!"

"What is it?" Carlos asked.

"It is so very, very terrible . . ." the queen said.

"Aaaah!" Smudge said.

The queen's eyes returned to the squirming dragon in her lap. "You want another bite, poopsie?"

"Mmhm." Smudge nodded.

The queen gave her poopsie another bite.

"Mom?" Impatience crept into Carlos's voice.

"Hm?" The queen looked up. "Oh! Yes! Terrible news, Carlos. Just terrible." And she went back to rubbing Smudge's belly.

Much to Carlos's relief, a new voice

entered the conversation. "Ah, good morning, son." It was King Carmine. He had made the long journey from the throne-room entrance without being noticed. "Did your mother tell you everything?"

"No," Carlos said.

The king looked to his queen. "Cora?"

"Hm?" The queen was scratching behind Smudge's ears.

"Aaaah!" Smudge said.

"Here you are, babycakes," the queen said.

The king rolled his eyes. "The dragon can hold his own ice cream, Cora."

"Oh, I know," the queen cooed, but she showed no sign of handing the fudgesicle to Smudge.

The king stood there for a long, indecisive moment. Then he rubbed his eyes as if they hurt. He looked tired. The king always looked *a little* tired, but today his light-brown, wrinkly skin made his face look like a used paper bag.

"Let's walk and talk, son," he said finally.

So they did, walking back down the long

ribbon of carpet, out of the throne room, and down the winding castle hallways. King Carmine's brisk pace and long, lanky legs forced Carlos to practically run alongside him.

"Your mother is a wonderful woman," the king began. "The most wonderful woman I have ever known. But pets . . . kind of distract her from . . . well, *everything*."

Carlos shrugged. "So what do you want me for?"

The king took a deep breath. "I have just heard that Princess Pinky has been kidnapped."

Carlos knew of Princess Pinky, but he had never met her. She lived in Ever-After

Land, a kingdom that was a strong friend and ally of Faraway Kingdom. Many years ago, Faraway Kingdom and Ever-After Land agreed to always help each other in times of trouble.

A kidnapping was trouble.

"Do you know where Princess Pinky is?" Carlos asked.

The king nodded. "I have reliable information that she is being held captive in the Tallest Tower. I need you to rescue her."

The conversation had been leading to this moment, but the king's request still made Carlos's heart skip a beat. "Me?" He stopped in his tracks.

The king stopped, too. "Yes, of course. That's why your mother and I wanted to speak with you. Rescuing damsels in distress is the princeliest thing a prince can ever do. Now, let's keep moving, son. It's not a walk-and-talk if we're talking but not walking."

Carlos stayed frozen in place. "But . . . the Tallest Tower? The Tallest Tower is located on *Witch Island*."

"Yes," the king said.

"And Witch Island has witches," Carlos said.

"Not anymore, I don't think," the king said. "Maybe one witch."

"And Witch Island is surrounded by Witch Lake!" Carlos's voice grew louder.

"Yes," the king said.

"Which might have more witches!" Carlos's voice grew even louder.

"Witches don't live in lakes, son," the king said.

"But witches might live *near* lakes! Especially if the name of the lake is *Witch Lake*!" Carlos was really loud now.

"Take the dragon," the king said. "Dragons can easily defeat witches."

"Oh, come on!" Carlos dialed his voice up to eleven. "Have you ever seen Smudge in action? All he does all day is sleep and eat ice cream!"

The king sighed. The king often sighed, but he sighed more often than usual when discussing Smudge. "Take him with you anyway. A walk will do him good. All that ice cream has made him too heavy to fly. He hasn't been able to reach the chandeliers for days now."

"But *Daaaad*!" Carlos's voice slipped into a whine that even he found annoying.

The king's eyebrows knitted together. "No, sir. No whining," the king said slowly. "You may whine when I ask you to clean your room. You may whine when your mother makes us eat Brussels sprouts. But you may *not* whine when a young woman's life is in danger. Your problems do not *begin* to compare to Princess Pinky's problems. Do you understand me?"

Carlos did understand. He stared down at his shoes. He felt his face get red.

The king put a gentle hand on Carlos's shoulder. His tone softened. "You can do this, son. I know you can. I wouldn't ask you if I had the slightest doubt in my mind. Your last adventure showed me how brave and resourceful you are."

"But why me?" Carlos's voice trembled a little. "Why not Gilbert the Gallant?"

It was a good question. Gilbert the Gallant was the prince of Ever-After Land. Princess Pinky was his younger sister. Gilbert was older, stronger, braver, and princelier than Carlos could ever be. He had even been profiled in a recent issue of *Better Castles & Hedge Mazes* magazine.

"Prince Gilbert would do it if he could," the king explained, "but he's overseas attending college. He's a new freshman at Princeton University."

Then the king did something that Carlos absolutely hated.

"Please," the king said. He said it so sweetly, so kindly, and so Charmingly that Carlos could only say one thing in reply:

"Okay."

CHAPTER 3

"Could be worse," Smudge volunteered.

"How?" Carlos asked. On his trudge to the royal barn, Carlos spotted a pinecone resting on the ground. He aimed a swift, frustrated kick at it but missed it completely. This made Carlos even more frustrated than before. "Now I probably won't be able to go to the Zimmerman bar mitzvah."

Carlos noticed an acorn by his feet and kicked at it even harder than the pinecone. He hit it, but just barely. It only bounced a few times before skittering off the trail. It was still very unsatisfying. "So instead of doing something I love, I have to save some princess I don't

even know from a tower a million miles high on an island a million miles away because her stupid older brother decided to go to college in New Jersey." Carlos kicked another acorn, but his aim was bad, and it rolled no more than five or six feet away. "So how can it be worse?"

"You could have to walk there," Smudge said.

The dragon had a point. Their destination was miles away. It was much too far to walk. To get to Witch Lake, Carlos planned to ride Cornelius, the royal horse. Smudge planned to be pulled by Cornelius in the royal horse cart.

Carlos had a long history of getting on

Cornelius's nerves, but he had worked hard to get on the horse's good side. Every morning, Carlos got up early to feed Cornelius the finest oats and carrots he could find. The horse, in turn, had recently stopped giving Carlos the stink eye.

That was real progress.

Cornelius was the fastest and strongest horse in all of Faraway Kingdom. He would be able to get Carlos and Smudge to Witch Lake in no time at all.

Carlos did the math in his head. With Cornelius's speed and a bit of luck, Carlos and Smudge might be able to reach the lake, get to the island, avoid the witch, rescue the princess, and get back home just in time to *maybe* catch the Zimmerman bar mitzvah.

It was possible, but it was a long shot.

A *long* long shot.

As he shoved open the barn door, Carlos felt frustrated all over again. Spotting a rock by the entrance, he gave it a ferocious kick. Unlike the pinecone and acorns, Carlos's foot hit its target right on the money, and the rock flew as if it were shot from a cannon. It ricocheted off one of the barn's support beams. It launched itself toward Cornelius's stall.

And it smacked Cornelius on the butt.

Suddenly the barn was alive with enraged whinnies, snorts, and thunderous kicks.

Cornelius, his ears flattened and mouth foaming with fury, lurched toward the stall door. He came nose-to-nose with Carlos.

"Sorry! I-I'm really sorry!" Carlos stammered as he fell backward into a bale of hay. "It w-was an accident."

Cornelius's stink eye had never been stinkier.

◆ ◆ ◆

"It's a nice, nice day for a long, long walk!" Smudge sang as he and Carlos walked toward the distant horizon. "It's not so loooong when it's so niiiice. With a frieeeeend!"

"Mm," Carlos grumbled.

"Cheer up," Smudge chirped. "I'll turn your frown upside down!"

"Hold on," Carlos protested. "*I'm* the jester. I'm the one who is supposed to turn frowns upside down."

"Then do it! I'll frown, and you turn it!" Smudge frowned, but his wagging tail didn't make the frown very convincing.

"Want me to juggle?" Carlos reached for the three knives on his belt.

"No! Tell a joke!" Smudge beamed. (He forgot that he was supposed to stay frowny.) "A joke about dragons!"

"Okay." Carlos thought for a moment. "Knock-knock."

"Who's there?" Smudge asked.

"Dragon."

"Dragon who?"

"Quit dragon your feet; we have a ten-mile hike ahead of us," Carlos said.

Smudge giggled. "That's funny! You de-frowned me!" Then Smudge pondered the punch line. "Is it really ten miles to Witch Lake?" he asked.

Carlos nodded. And the two of them plodded on.

◆ ◆ ◆

"I'm tired, CC. Can you carry me?" Smudge asked.

Carlos raised an eyebrow. "Are you kidding? You're too big to carry."

The dragon harrumphed at this news. "It's the ice cream. It makes my belly big."

"You'd be too big to carry even if you didn't eat ice cream."

"I need to eat ice cream, CC. I need ice cream to cool my hot bref."

"You could always cool your breath with ice."

"I *do* cool my bref with ice," Smudge explained. "*Creamy* ice."

◆　◆　◆

"What do you see in the clouds, CC?" Smudge wondered dreamily as they stretched in the grass.

Carlos squirmed a little. A rock was

poking between his shoulder blades. "I don't see anything. There are no clouds today."

The dragon burped a few puffs of gray smoke up in the air. "*Now* what do you see?"

Carlos studied Smudge's work for a moment. "I see a rubber chicken," he decided.

"I see ice cream," Smudge replied.

◆ ◆ ◆

Carlos and Smudge scrambled over a ridge of boulders.

"When you rescue the princess, are you going to kiss her?" Smudge asked.

"Ew, no," Carlos said. "Why would I kiss her?"

Smudge shrugged. "I thought princes were kissy."

"Well, jesters are *not* kissy," Carlos grumbled. "Not kissy *at all*."

◆ ◆ ◆

"Are we there yet?" Smudge asked. It felt as if the two of them had been walking for hours, because they had been.

"Do you need another break?" Carlos asked. Carlos sure needed one.

"Maybe a little one." Smudge plopped down on his big, scaly bottom. "Hey, CC?"

Carlos sat down, too. "Hm?"

"Why do you think a witch kidnapped Princess Pinky?"

"We don't know if a *witch* kidnapped her," Carlos said.

"But the princess is on Witch Island," Smudge reasoned. "So it's *probably* a witch who did it, right?"

The idea made Carlos's chest feel tight.

"Do you think the princess will be an ingredient in a witch's potion?" Smudge asked.

"Ingredient?!" Carlos gulped. "In a potion?"

"You know, like the way witches use newt

eyes or rabbit ears? Do you think a witch might use the princess's eyes or ears in a witch potion?"

Instead of answering, Carlos sprang to his feet. "Okay! Break's over. Let's keep moving."

◆ ◆ ◆

Carlos never would have imagined that a place called Witch Lake could be such a welcome sight. Upon arriving, he was unable to walk another step. He dropped to his knees at the lapping shoreline, cupped his hands, and slurped up water until the front of his shirt was soaked through.

He squinted across the water's surface and found the island, which was partly hidden by mist. The tower upon it reached into the sky.

"That's where we're going," he said. "Now all we have to do is figure out how to get there."

"We could swim," Smudge suggested.

"Can *you* swim?" Carlos asked.

"No," Smudge admitted. "But I could take lessons!"

Carlos sighed. "I think we need another way, Smudge."

"How about a PINK BOAT?" Smudge asked.

Carlos sighed again. "Where are we going
to find—?"

Carlos turned his head and found the answer to his question. Peacefully bobbing off
to one side was a pink paddleboat shaped to
resemble a flamingo. A long neck sprouted

from the bow and arched over the water. A smile was painted on a black beak. The eyes twinkled invitingly.

It was a beautiful and cheerful sight, but it made Carlos uneasy. The sign stuck into the ground beside the boat made Carlos even *more* uneasy. It read:

Free Transportation to Witch Island

Is this a trap? Carlos wondered. *Is this boat an evil witch trick?*

Carlos was having a difficult time thinking it over. It's difficult to think things over when a skipping dragon is shouting things like "Wowie!" and "Look at the bird boat!" and "Pink is my favorite color!"

"It is a nice boat," Carlos said, "but I don't know if we should . . ."

Carlos trailed off when he realized he was talking to nobody.

"WHEEEE!" Smudge had run to the flamingo and was tumbling into one of the seats. The boat bobbed under Smudge's weight, making the flamingo's head nod in approval.

"I'm the captain!" Smudge announced. "I call the captain's chair! C'mon, CC! What'cha waiting for? Let's go go go!"

CHAPTER 4

"Do you think there are sea monsters in here?" Smudge squinted into the water, forgetting for about the fiftieth time that he was supposed to be doing half of the pedaling.

"No," Carlos replied, but the more honest

answer was "I hope not." For all Carlos knew, a witch could have created a sea monster for this lake. A witch could have also trained the sea monster to attack pink flamingo boats.

Carlos focused on the rhythmic *ga-splush* of the waves. He tried to push the idea of sea monsters out of his mind.

"Do you know any sea monster jokes?" Smudge asked.

Carlos did. "What does a sea monster eat for dinner?"

"What?" Smudge asked.

"Fish and ships." The punch line made Carlos's gut twist into a knot.

Smudge frowned. "I don't get it."

"Don't worry. It's not a very good joke." Carlos made a point of not looking into the water, but that left him no choice but to look at Witch Island, which double-knotted his gut. The Tallest Tower triple-knotted it.

As the island grew near, however, Carlos was surprised by how un-witchy it looked. In fact, the island was inviting. It was thick with lush greenery. Its shores were gently sloped and free from hull-damaging rocks. Songbirds chirped in its treetops. The place even smelled nice—fresh and breezy, like clothesline laundry.

But Carlos knew looks (and sounds and smells) could be deceiving.

Don't let your guard down, Carlos thought. *This is Witch Island. A witch lives here. And that witch has kidnapped a princess.*

The bottom of the flamingo boat crunched against the island's sandy shore.

"Okay," Carlos said. "Smudge, before we get started, we need a game plan."

"Cool!" Smudge exclaimed.

"First part of the game plan is that we need to keep really quiet," Carlos said.

"Cool," Smudge whispered.

"That's all I have so far," Carlos admitted.

"It's good." Smudge nodded. "I like it."

Carlos and Smudge tiptoed across the beach and squeezed between the trees.

Most of them were pines, so there were no crunchy leaves underfoot to announce their arrival. A few minutes later, the two of them reached a flat, sandy clearing. In the middle of the clearing stood a cylindrical tower made from black stone that was polished to a high shine. At the very top, barely visible from where they stood, was a large window.

Carlos leaned toward Smudge's ear. "Look for a door."

Still on tippy-toes, the two circled the tower. There was no door. They circled it another three times just to make sure.

Nope. Still no door.

"Any more game plan?" Smudge asked.

"Maybe there's a tunnel?" Carlos wished he sounded more confident, but his tone matched how he felt. "Let's spread out and look for a secret entrance."

Moving in slow circles, Carlos kept his eyes to the ground, sweeping the sand with his feet in case it was hiding a hole or a hatch.

Nothing.

Smudge did the same, sweeping and poking at the ground with his snout and tail. He wasn't having any luck, either. As Carlos eyed a tree stump with suspicion, Smudge searched behind the tower, out of Carlos's line of sight.

"Oh, hai!" Smudge shouted. (This was a clear violation of the game plan.)

Carlos nearly leapt out of his skin. "Shh! Did you find something?"

Then he heard Smudge scream.

CHAPTER 5

Carlos fumbled for the juggling knives in his belt.

"I'm coming, Smudge!" he shouted, and immediately he wished he hadn't. He'd just announced his actions to whatever horrible thing was concealed behind the tower. His mistake made his fingers tremble. One of his knives plunked into the dirt.

He managed to hold on to the other two. Clutching one knife in each hand, he raced around the tower in a tight counterclockwise circle, practically brushing up against the curved wall with his left shoulder.

He was terrified of what he might find. A witch, certainly. Smudge might be under a spell! Or in great pain! Or dying! Or being used as an ingredient in a potion!

Carlos could feel his heart pounding in his ears.

He skidded around the bend and saw Smudge racing right toward *him*, smiling, skipping, and dancing around the tower in a tight *clockwise* circle, practically brushing up against the curved wall with his *right* shoulder.

"CC!" Smudge called.

"GAAAH!" Carlos cried.

Carlos pushed off from the wall to avoid a collision. At once he lost his footing and face-planted into the sand. Both knives flew from his hands and skidded into the weeds.

"CC!" Smudge shouted. "CC! You okay?"

Smudge's eyes were wide with alarm. His skipping-and-dancing engine, however, was still running. It's difficult to be alarmed and joyful at the same time, but Smudge pulled it off.

Carlos spat some sand out of his mouth before answering. *"Pthpthpthpth!* I'm okay. *Ptoo!* Are you okay?"

"Oh, yeah, yeah, yeah! I'm good! I'm really

good!" Now that Smudge knew Carlos was unhurt, his smile returned. His skipping and dancing shifted into a higher gear.

"Why on earth did you scream?" Carlos asked.

"Because I found something awesome!" The dragon held up his hand to show off a gray something about the size of a dinner roll. "Can I have this, CC? Can I?"

Carlos fixed his gaze on the object. "Is that a rock?"

"Yeah!"

"A rock with eyes glued on it," Carlos said.

"Uh-huh! And the eyes move! Look!" Smudge shook it. The eyes jiggled, as if the rock didn't know whether it was coming or going. "Can I keep it? Can I?"

Carlos tried to mimic Smudge's enthusiasm, but his heart wasn't in it. "That's cute," he muttered as he pulled himself into a standing position. Both of his knees cracked. "Where did you get that thing?"

"From her!" Smudge pointed.

Carlos's eyes followed the direction of Smudge's hand to find a plump, elderly woman, her gray hair tied into a loose bun. She straddled a large tricycle with fat tires. Almost elfin in size, she was barely able to see above the wire basket attached to her handlebars. The basket spilled over with rocks, driftwood, and leafy branches.

Tied to the basket was a hand-lettered sign. It read: **witch craft**

"The witch!" Carlos slapped the rock out of Smudge's hand.

"Hey!" Smudge protested. "My rock!"

"Don't touch it!" Carlos shouted. "It's an evil witch rock!"

"But I named it." Smudge pouted.

Carlos searched his belt for another juggling knife, but he had already dropped them all.

The mystery woman began to pedal. Her tricycle maneuvered through the sand with surprising ease.

As she drew closer, Carlos stared. He found her eyes unnervingly sparkly, cheerful, and unoffended by his witchy accusations. That was a sure sign she was a witch. Only a witch would not be offended at being called a witch.

"You liked my boat?" she asked. Her voice sounded a little dusty but not unpleasant.

"That was your boat?" Carlos asked.

"Of course," the woman said. "People have to get here somehow. Might as well make it easy for them."

The woman continued to roll toward him.

Carlos saw that her face was free of warts. Everyone knew that witch faces were supposed to be warty. *That can only mean one thing*, Carlos thought. *This witch is so skilled in witchcraft that she can de-wart her face! She is the witchiest witch ever!*

"Don't come any closer, you witch!" Carlos shouted.

"Settle yourself, sonny," she replied. "I am not a witch."

That sounded like something a witch would say. Carlos searched the ground for a weapon, but the only thing within reach was Smudge's rock, which stared up at him with its evil, lifeless, googly eyes. Carlos didn't dare touch it.

"Well, that's not *entirely* true," the old woman added. She stopped the bike a few feet from where Carlos stood. She slowly, carefully slid off the seat. "What I *should* say is, I'm not a witch *anymore*. I am a once-witch."

Carlos furrowed his brow. "What's a *one switch*?"

She spoke more slowly. "Once. Witch. Just like it says on my—" A quick glance at her tricycle basket stopped her short. "Oh, dear! I see your problem now." She pushed aside some twigs that were covering parts of the "witch craft" sign. It now read:

Ethel's once-witch crafts

"I'm Ethel," she said. "I sold my cauldrons and flying brooms many years ago to start a new business. Now I make and sell souvenirs."

"Oh" was all Carlos could muster.

"The flamingo boat really brings in the

tourists," she went on. "So! Would you like a Witch Island souvenir?"

"No, thank you," said Carlos.

"Yes, thank you!" said Smudge.

"Oh," Carlos said. "Right. I guess we'll take the rock."

Ethel beamed. "Great! Ten dollars."

"Wait. What?" Carlos said. "Ten dollars for a *rock*?"

"Pleeeease . . . ?" Smudge begged.

"No, Smudge," Carlos said. "That's too expensive."

But Ethel was nothing if not a good salesperson. "It's well worth the price. That rock is made from the finest rock."

"I named him Rocky!" reported Smudge.

"You can name another rock Rocky," Carlos said.

But Smudge wasn't ready to let the matter drop. He adopted a high, squeaky voice. *"Pleeeease buy me,"* Smudge said in Rocky's voice. *"I am so worth it! I be ya best friend."*

Carlos rubbed his eyes as if they hurt.

"Okay, okay—I'll buy the rock," Carlos said to Ethel. "But *only* if you release Princess Pinky!"

"Who's Princess Pinky?" Ethel asked.

"Oh, come on!" Carlos was at his wit's end. "She's the girl in your tower!"

"My tower?" Ethel peered up at the tower's distant window. She scratched her head, allowing a few strands of tangled hair to escape her bun. "I haven't been in that tower in years. No one has."

"Well, *someone's* up there," Carlos said. "How do you get to the top?"

"A magic word reveals a staircase," Ethel explained.

"Okay," Carlos said. "So what's the magic word?"

Ethel sighed. "I don't remember it anymore."

"You don't remember it anymore?!" Carlos shouted.

Ethel cleared her throat. Her mouth twitched into an apologetic smile. "It's been a long time since I used magic words. A very long time."

"Does anyone else know the magic word?" Carlos asked.

Ethel shook her head.

Carlos stared up at the distant window and did his best to make sense of it all.

If no one knows how to get to the top of the tower, he wondered, *how can anyone be at the top of the tower?*

Then Carlos wondered something else: *Could the tower be empty?*

"Hey, Smudge, can you fly to the window and see if anyone is up there?" Carlos asked.

"Will do!" Smudge flapped his rubbery bat wings.

He flapped and flapped, harder and harder and faster and faster, until Smudge,

Carlos, and Ethel found themselves in the middle of a blinding storm of dust.

When the dust finally settled, Smudge was still on the ground.

Smudge stared down at his toes. "Maybe I should eat ice that's less creamy," he said miserably.

Carlos petted Smudge's snout. "It's okay. There are other ways to find out if the princess is up there."

Carlos cupped his hands around his mouth and shouted into the sky. **"HEL-LOOOOOO!"**

A dark-haired head poked out of the distant window.

"It's her! She's there!" Carlos practically leapt for joy. He cupped his hands around his mouth again. **"IT'S YOU! YOU'RE THERE!"**

The girl said something in reply, but her words got lost in the wind.

"DON'T WORRY! I AM HERE TO HELP YOU!" Carlos shouted so loudly that his throat protested under the strain.

Again, the girl spoke. Again, her words didn't reach the ground.

"Did she say 'help'?" Carlos asked, his voice now taking on a slight rasp. "I think I heard 'help.'"

"I heard that, too!" Smudge agreed. "I also heard 'own.'"

Ethel nodded. "I think she said 'alone.'"

"That's it! *Alone!* She's *alone*! And she needs *help*!" Carlos turned to the once-witch. "Are you *sure* you don't remember the magic word that gives the tower its steps?"

Ethel shrugged. "I'm trying. . . ."

"Think, Ethel," Carlos said. "We just need that one magic word!"

The imprisoned girl let out yet another shout.

Carlos stared up at her. The princess looked angry and desperate.

"I'm sorry, sonny," Ethel sighed. "But there is only one way to get to the top of that tower. You're gonna have to climb."

The word *climb* stopped him cold. He looked at Ethel to see if she was serious. She was.

His gaze returned to the distant window.

In that moment, Carlos had an overwhelming urge to throw up.

CHAPTER 6

"Are you sure climbing is the only way to get into the tower?" Carlos asked.

It was.

Though the stones in the tower were smooth and polished to a high shine, the narrow seams where the stones met offered places to hold on. At least, Carlos hoped they did. He traced a seam at about shoulder height with his left hand and found a spot where he could wriggle his fingers inside. With his right hand, he reached for a seam above his head and discovered another handhold.

The toe of his left boot squeezed into a seam at knee height.

Maybe this *was* possible. He pulled himself off the ground and pressed flat against the wall. The coolness of the stone was oddly refreshing. He preferred it to all the walking and pedaling and sweating that had happened earlier in the day.

He slowly lifted his right boot, tracing

the wall until a bumpy spot revealed itself as another foothold.

"I think I can do this," Carlos said. He cast a glance down at Smudge and Ethel.

As he did so, a wave of dizziness washed over him like a waterfall. His chest grew tight. He gulped for air. His vision began to blur.

"You afraid of heights, sonny?" Ethel asked.

"I don't know," Carlos replied.

"You're only three feet off the ground," Ethel said.

Carlos's feet might have been three feet off the ground, but his head was *eight* feet off the ground, and it felt much, *much* higher.

And his head still had about four hundred ninety-two feet to go.

He clamped his eyes shut and clenched the wall until his fingertips felt as if they were on fire.

"You can do it, CC!" Smudge cheered.

"Can you do it?" Ethel asked.

Carlos was about to say no. Before the word could reach his lips, however, the dizziness vanished as quickly as it had come. He could breathe again.

That was strange. Somehow or other, he had shaken off his fears.

Until he opened his eyes again.

"Whoa!" he shouted. "Whoa!" He closed his eyes. Once again, the feelings passed.

"I can do this," Carlos said, "as long as I don't look."

Ethel raised an eyebrow. "Is that a good idea?"

Of course it wasn't a good idea. It was a *terrible* idea. But it was also the *only* idea.

Carlos's left hand blindly crept up the wall in search of another seam. When he found one, he held on. His right hand followed. His left foot slid searchingly along the wall until it dug into the first crevice it found. Then up Carlos went, sliding against polished stone.

Slowly, steadily, with only his sense of touch leading him, Carlos pulled himself higher and higher.

The higher he went, the breezier it became, with an occasional gust blowing his sweaty forehead dry. He had no idea how far he had gone or how much farther he had to go. He didn't dare look to find out, but he had clues. Smudge's cries of support had nearly faded into nothing. The strong winds and the absence of birdsong told him he was well above the tree line.

Yet he wasn't tired. In fact, he found it exhilarating. He was climbing a tower!

The longer he climbed, the easier it became. He grew familiar with the building—how large its stones were and where to find its seams. He learned the best ways to hold on to those seams and how to best support his weight when pulling himself up.

Right foot, left hand, right hand, left foot, and pull up. Over and over and over again. It became a kind of game.

Right foot, left hand, right hand, left foot, and pull up.

Right foot, left hand, right hand, left foot . . .

Left foot . . .

Left . . . foot . . .

Uh-oh.

The toe of Carlos's left boot was stuck in a crack.

He wiggled his ankle back and forth and up and down, but the boot wouldn't budge.

It was really stuck in there.

Despite the aggressive breeze, a fresh sheen of sweat formed on Carlos's forehead. His palms grew wet and slippery.

He very slowly removed his left hand from the wall to wipe it on his shirt, which didn't do much good. His palm got sweaty again almost immediately after he dried it.

Sweat dribbled into his eye and began to sting.

He blinked the sweat away. In that instant, he saw *everything*.

The vibrant blue of the sky.

The tree line far below.

The ground *even farther* below.

The much-too-tiny cracks and crevices he held on to.

The wind felt stronger now, strong enough to shove him off his perch.

His eyes blurred. His chest grew tight. His breath left him.

Carlos shut his eyes, but what he had seen stayed in his mind.

Don't think about it, don't think about it, don't think about it.

But trying not to think about it made Carlos think about it even *more*.

He felt his weight shift.

And then he felt himself begin to fall.

CHAPTER 7

Something pressed against Carlos's back. A hand? He didn't dare open his eyes to find out. His cheek, once again, found the cool comfort of the tower wall.

Something snaked itself around his chest.

Someone said, "Sit tight. I'll be right back."

And he heard movement by his right ear.

Whatever was around his chest had to be rope, Carlos realized. It tightened up under his armpits and squeezed him like an anaconda. His back cracked in three places.

"Oof," he said.

Then up he went. His cheek squeaked against the stone. His left foot wriggled out of the boot, which remained behind, still stuck in the tower's wall.

It was a jerky, unsteady rise, which made

Carlos think that he would fall at any moment. His teeth clenched so hard that his jaw hurt. His toes curled in fear, making his feet ache. And yet, he kept going up. The side of his face announced every inch of the journey:

Squeeeeeak.

After what felt like forever, Carlos was pulled through a window. He tumbled onto a stone floor. He never wanted to move from that spot ever again.

"You can open your eyes now," the voice said.

For a few long moments, Carlos saw only

a blur. The blur of a girl. The late-afternoon sun streamed through her wild, black, curly hair.

An angel, Carlos thought.

The blurry angel put her hands on her hips. "What are you doing up here, dummy?"

That didn't sound very angelic.

"I . . . I . . ." Carlos began. "I'm here to save you."

"My hero," she replied. "Don't you understand plain English? I kept yelling and yelling that I don't *want* your help. I kept telling you to leave me alone!"

"*That's* what you were saying?" Carlos let out a groan.

"Why were you helping me, anyway?" the girl asked.

"You've been kidnapped," Carlos said.

Now it was the girl's turn to groan. "Great. As soon as I go missing for, like, two minutes, my mom and dad freak out and tell the world I'm kidnapped. One time I took a walk around the block without telling them. By the time I got back to the castle, my picture was on a half million cartons of milk."

"So you're Princess Pinky?" Carlos asked.

"No. I'm just Pinky."

"That's what I said. Princess Pinky," Carlos said.

"Don't call me 'princess,'" she said sharply.

"But I thought you were a princess," Carlos said.

"I *am* a princess. Okay?" Pinky said. "I *am*. I just . . ."

She didn't finish her thought, so Carlos finished it for her. "You'd just rather not be?"

"Something like that," she said.

Carlos understood. "How did you get up here?" he asked.

"I climbed up. Just like you did," Pinky replied. "Well, no, *not* just like you did. When *I* climbed up, I didn't need to be rescued."

Carlos's eyes finally came into focus. For the first time, he got a good look at Pinky. What struck him immediately was that she had a very strong resemblance to her older brother, Gilbert. She had the same confident eyes; same flawless, ebony skin; same high cheekbones; and same elegant nose. But, unlike Gilbert, Pinky didn't seem very royal. Her paint-splattered overalls weren't very princess-like, but her lack of traditional royal-ness went beyond what she wore.

It's the way she carries herself, Carlos decided. Gilbert always stood ramrod straight, his every move as elegant as a dancer's. Pinky's posture, on the other hand, was more like a permanent, defiant shrug. Even wearing the fanciest of gowns, Pinky would probably still look more rebel than royal.

"Stop staring at me," Pinky said. She ran her hand through her hair, revealing a hidden streak that was dyed bright pink.

"Sorry," Carlos said. Instead, he stared

at his surroundings. The room was small and would look like a prison cell if it weren't for the brilliant light from the window and the many, many paintings on the wall. "Wow!" Carlos said. "Did you paint all these?"

"Yup," Pinky said.

They were landscapes mostly, but there were also still lifes of neatly arranged flowers, nuts, berries, and other objects. The colors were unnaturally bright and alive, the brushstrokes aggressive and thick with paint. Carlos never knew that a bowl of fruit could be so . . . was *exciting* the word? As his eyes jumped from one picture to the

next, he couldn't come up with a better description.

"Wow," Carlos said again.

"This is my secret art studio." Pinky's voice grew a shade bitter. "Well, it *was* secret until today."

"Don't worry," Carlos said. "I won't tell anyone."

"Yeah, right." She moved toward the window. An easel stood near the ledge, holding a blank canvas. Pinky busied herself with some small tubes, squirting blobs of paint onto the outer edge of a palette.

"Why is your art studio secret?" Carlos asked.

"Because I am a *princess*." The last word dripped with scorn.

"I don't get it," Carlos said.

She turned to meet his gaze. Her face was now a shade of crimson. "I've been told that painting is a waste of time. My parents would rather have me walk around with a book on my head. That way I can learn to walk like I have a stick up my butt, like my oh-so perfect brother."

"Ah," Carlos said.

"They'd rather have me practice my cursive writing," Pinky said, "even though *nobody* writes in cursive anymore."

"I understand," Carlos said.

"They'd rather have me work on my table manners," Pinky said, "to make sure I don't eat soup with a fork."

"You eat soup with a fork?" Carlos asked.

"When soup is chunky, it's *fun* to eat it with a fork!" Pinky said. "Don't judge me!"

Carlos raised his hands. "I'm not. Really, I'm not."

And he wasn't.

"I'm not the only person of royal birth who has a secret life, you know," she said. "For every obedient prince like you and Gilbert, there is someone like me. Someone who wants to do something different."

She stared out the window and studied

the setting sun. "You might not believe me, but it's true. I've even heard of a prince who goes around telling jokes like a jester."

"Wait! What?" Carlos's eyes went wide. "You have?"

She nodded. "He's the talk of the kingdom."

Carlos suddenly felt light-headed. It wasn't the same light-headed he'd felt while clinging to the side of the tower. It was a *good* light-headed. An *amazing* light-headed.

"The talk of the kingdom?" Carlos asked. "He's, like . . . *famous*?"

"Shh," Pinky said. "I need to focus. I've

been waiting all day to paint this sunset, and the sky is almost exactly the way I want it."

Carlos pulled himself off the floor (both of his knees cracked) and joined Pinky at the window. He was greeted by a remarkable sight.

The sky was streaked with shades of orange, pink, and purple, which reflected onto the glittering water of Witch Lake. The pine trees that surrounded the tower lit up in shades of bright green and yellow. Carlos never knew nature could contain so much beauty.

"Wow," he whispered.

"This is why I come here," Pinky whispered back.

For a long moment, neither one of them spoke. They just watched.

A noise behind them, a sharp **WHOOSH,** broke the spell.

Pinky and Carlos whirled around just in time to see a section of the wall melt before their eyes. The paintings hanging on it clattered to the ground.

Where the wall had been was an open doorway. And through the doorway was a staircase spiraling downward.

Moments later, Carlos heard familiar clickita-clickitas.

"CC! Good news! Good news!" Smudge shouted. "Ethel remembered the magic

word! She remembered the magic word!"
Smudge's head poked through the doorway.
"The magic word was *please*."

Smudge noticed Pinky. "Oh, hai!"

"Um. Hi," Pinky replied.

Carlos realized that introductions were

in order. "Pinky, this is Smudge. Smudge, this is Pinky."

"Hai," Smudge said again. "And CC! I got even *gooder* news! Ethel says her witch memory is coming back! *And* she can come up with a spell to get us to the Zimmerman bar mitzvah in two shakes of a Smudge's tail!"

"She can?" Carlos asked.

"You'll be able to do your jestering after all!" Smudge said.

Pinky's eyebrows shot upward. Her gaze shifted from Smudge to Carlos. "*You're* the jester prince?"

Carlos nodded.

"Wow," she said. She looked at Carlos as if she hadn't really noticed him before that moment.

Smudge was practically bouncing off the wall. "We gotta hurry, CC! It's way after five o'clock! We'll barely make it!"

"I don't think so, Smudge," Carlos said. "I mean, I already lost my juggling stuff. And a boot. And it's getting dark. I think . . ." He paused. "I think I'd rather stay here and watch the sunset." Carlos turned to Pinky. "Do you mind if I stay a little longer? I'll keep quiet. So will Smudge."

"Oh, yes! I am a very quiet dragon!" Smudge announced not very quietly.

Pinky smiled a warm, crooked smile before turning back to her canvas. "Yeah, okay," she said. "*If* you're quiet."

She gazed at the sunset. The sky was an explosion of color.

"That's what I've been waiting for," Pinky said. "It's perfect."

Her brush swirled paint on her palette. Magenta streaks flew across her canvas.

Carlos and Smudge took it all in.

Smudge tugged on Carlos's shirtsleeve. Carlos positioned his ear next to Smudge's mouth.

"She's a good artist," Smudge whispered.

"Yes," Carlos whispered back.

Smudge leaned closer to Carlos's ear. "Did we make a new bestest friend?"

"I don't know," Carlos whispered.

"We did." Smudge nodded. "And that's good. There's always room for more bestest friends."

"Yes, there is," Carlos agreed.

And, without another word, he marveled as Pinky turned her surroundings into something colorful and exciting and alive.

AN EXCLUSIVE INTERVIEW
WITH ROY L. HINUSS

Author of *Once Upon a Prank* and authorized
biographer of the Charming Royal Family

Thank you for agreeing to be interviewed, Mr. Hinuss.

It is my pleasure! You promised to pay me, yes?

Yes.

Then it really is my pleasure.

How did you become authorized biographer of the Charming Royal Family?

I was asked to be the authorized biographer because I am a gentleman and a man of many talents. For example, last year I put on *The Threepenny Opera* with a cast of wild raccoons. That had never been done before!

Did the audience like it?

The audience loved it! If they didn't get rabies.

People in the audience got rabies?

Some got rabies, yes.

How many got rabies?

All of them.

Is that the reason why you were named authorized biographer of the Charming Royal Family?

Certainly not. I am also a writer of great renown.

What did you write?

My most famous book is *For the Love of Donkeys*.
It describes the many political, cultural, and
artistic contributions donkeys have made
throughout history.

**Donkeys have made political, cultural,
and artistic contributions?**

No. Not really. It's not a very long book. My
editor suggested adding a lot of pictures.

**So the donkey book is the reason why you
were named authorized biographer . . . ?**

No. I was chosen because I am a successful
businessman.

Okay. A businessman. And what is your business?

I'm between businesses right now.

What *was* your business?

I ran a raccoon opera company.

Ah, yes. So you are the authorized biographer because . . . ?

No one else wanted to do it.

What does an authorized biographer of the Charming Royal Family do?

Well, the big thing is to learn the history of the Charming Royal Family.

Charmings have ruled Faraway Kingdom for the past two thousand years. That's a lot of history. I find that history makes me sleepy.

But you are an expert.
Oh, yes! I can tell you about every Charming who has ever lived.

Great! Let's talk a little about Prince Carlos.
Who?

The prince.
Who?

Prince Carlos Charles Charming.

Doesn't ring a bell.

You wrote books about him!

For the Love of Donkeys?

No! *Once Upon a Prank*!

Oh, *that* Prince Carlos! He isn't a donkey.

I know that!

I don't think he went to *The Threepenny Opera*,
either. Does Prince Carlos have rabies?

No.

Well, then, he missed a great show.

Can we talk about Prince Carlos, please?

You're paying me, aren't you?

Yes.

Then it is my pleasure.

As you know, Prince Carlos doesn't want to be a prince at all. Have there been other Charmings who didn't want to be princes or princesses?

Oh, yes. Prince Corky Charming XIII, born in 1812, didn't want to be a prince. He wanted to be a dinosaur. But he grew out of it when he turned three.

Do you think Prince Carlos's obsession with being a jester might make him the worst king in Faraway Kingdom's history?

If Carlos lives long enough to be king, he will not be the worst king in Faraway Kingdom's history. That honor must go to King Clyde Charming XXXVIII. He ruled Faraway Kingdom for four days in August 1492.

What made him such a bad king?

He didn't have a head.

Someone cut off his head?

No, he was born without a head. That made

things difficult. He couldn't give any orders because mouths are on people's heads. The king just sort of gurgled. Nobody had any idea what the guy was talking about.

The problem was eventually solved by King Clyde's wife, Queen Clio. She led the king over to an easy chair someplace out of the way and left him there to watch TV or whatever. And everyone just sort of forgot about him. Queen Clio ruled Faraway Kingdom for the next thirty years.

The people of Faraway Kingdom loved Queen Clio. King Clyde wasn't exactly a tough act to follow.

Mr. Hinuss?

Yes, sir.

Did that really happen?

The important thing is that it *could have* happened.

That is *not* the important thing.

You're right. The important thing is that you're paying me. You are still paying me, yes?

I suppose so.

Then it was nice to meet you.

Don't miss the first book in the

Prince Not-So Charming series,

Once Upon a Prank!

ABOUT THE AUTHOR

Roy L. Hinuss is the authorized biographer of the Charming Royal Family. He is also fond of the occasional fart joke. When he isn't writing about Prince Carlos Charles Charming's many adventures, he can be found cataloging his collection of celebrity toenail clippings.